The Icky Sticky Frog

Written by
Dawn Bentley

Designed and Illustrated by
Salina Yoon

Piggy Toes PRESS

On a pretty blue lake, on a big brown log sat a very quiet little green frog.
A fly flew by.
SHH! Frog didn't make a sound.
He just eyed the fly flying around.

WOOP! Out came Frog's tongue
so sticky and long, and . . .

SLURP! The fly was gone!

Just as Frog was swallowing the fly
a colorful beetle came crawling by.

SHH! Frog didn't make a sound.
He just eyed the beetle crawling around.

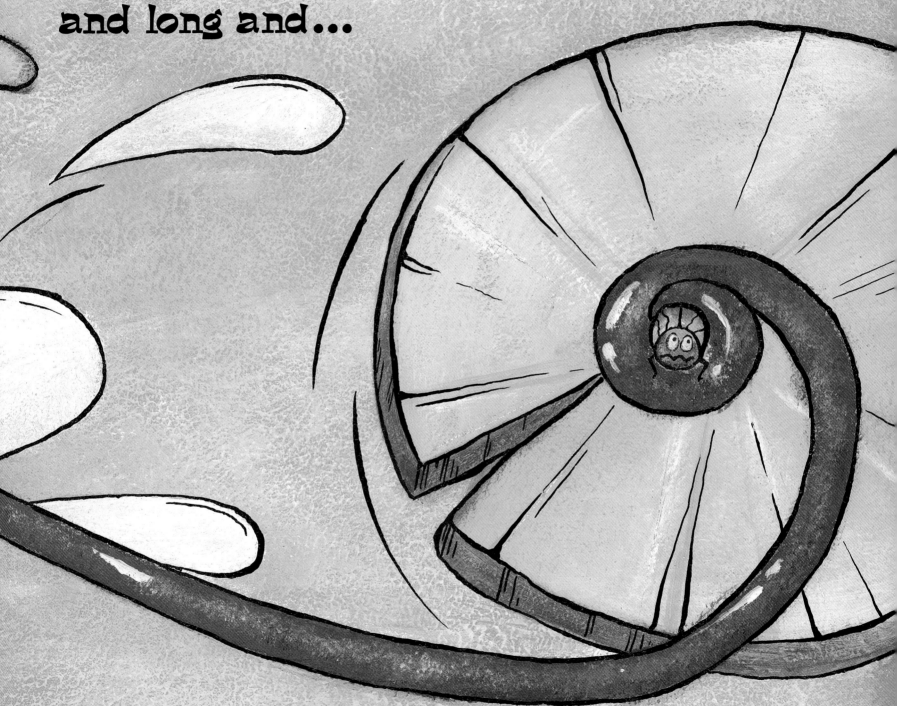

WOOP! Out came his tongue so sticky and long and...

SLURP! Now the beetle was gone.

The frog swallowed the beetle
like he swallowed the fly,
then a green grasshopper
came hopping by.

Frog swallowed the
grasshopper hopping by
like he swallowed the beetle
and he swallowed the fly,
and then he saw a pretty butterfly.

SHH! Frog didn't make a sound.
He just eyed the butterfly flying around.
WOOP! Out came Frog's tongue
so sticky and long and....